D0294936

For Angela
2000 5 9 7 1
MORAY COUNCIL
Department of Technical
& Leisure Services
JB

A Bear Tale

Robert Ingpen

Copyright © Robert Ingpen

First published 2000 by Thomas Lothian Pty Ltd,
Melbourne, Australia

This edition first published 2000 by
Happy Cat Books, Bradfield, Essex CO11 2UT

All rights reserved

A CIP catalogue record for this book is available
from the British Library

ISBN 1 899248 25 0

Designed by Robert Ingpen

Printed in Hong Kong by South China Printing

Happy Cat Books

As Ted the Bear sat with all the other toys in the corner of the bedroom, he thought about getting comfortable.

'I can sit up straight,' he said to nobody in particular. 'I can lie on my back, or on my front, but slumping is best. I do a slump because it sounds comfortable — I like the way it sounds.'

So he said it three times, quite loudly, 'Slump, slump, slump.'

Once someone saw him slumping and commented, 'What a wise old bear you seem to be.'

And, of course, Ted agreed he was, and felt pleased that the others noticed how wisely he slumped. To him it sounded rather good to be old and wise, particularly when you could also be comfortable.

He knew about old, because he had grown up gradually becoming old. His nose was worn, one eye was loose, a paw was bandaged and his growl had gone.

But he really needed to know what wise meant.

So he started asking about wisdom.

'How do you get it?' he questioned various toys. 'Where does it come from? What does it look like?'

None of the toys knew for sure, not even Joey the Dog.

Joey said that he had once heard that owls were wise, and so they would probably know what wisdom was and how you could get some. He advised Ted, 'If you go and talk to the owls, they will surely be able to answer your questions.'

The owls were a collection of ornaments who lived in a semi-circle on a table in the far corner, right across the bedroom. Their owner had collected them on her visits to worldly places. She had arranged them in such a way that they might be expected to answer questions, give advice and sometimes make judgements.

There were owls from everywhere — from
Mexico, England, Germany and even
Taiwan — owls made of pottery, china,
wood and cloth.

With quite a big effort, Ted left his home in the corner and made his way as best he could across the bedroom to the owls' table.

Without any greeting or preamble, he addressed the collection of owls. 'If I am a wise bear, how can I tell?'

There was no answer, so he repeated the question.

Still no answer.

'Perhaps they are dumb, or deaf,' he thought, and was just about to ask for the third time, in a louder voice, when the fluffy young German owl spoke softly.

'We can't tell you.'

'Why not?' said Ted, feeling a little uncomfortable and sorry that he had left home. He felt even worse when there was silence once again.

After a long while, the brown English owl
with a ring in his nose began what was to
be a long, rambling, speech. 'We can't tell
you,' he repeated. 'We can't tell you
because we do not know. We owls have
been seeking the answers to all the
questions about wisdom since Han Owl
was born. That was ages ago, and we still
don't know.'

Then he went on and on about looking
for wisdom, until he finally interested Ted
by saying something he could understand.

'We *can* tell you this,' the English owl
announced. 'We owls are often told that if
we go to a place crowded with toys, like
dolls, dogs and bears and things, we will be
told the answers. But that, of course, is
nonsense.'

'Why is that nonsense?' said Ted, now feeling rather hurt. He tried to comfort himself by slumping, but English Owl made that difficult by saying, 'Because they — the toys — could not possibly know anything. It would be a waste of time asking.'

Ted was just on the point of getting up and leaving the company of owls when he was surprised to hear himself say, 'How do you *know* that we toys would not know?'

He felt good challenging the owl.

'Well,' said a voice from the back of the group. It was Han Owl, the ancient Chinese bowl owl, and he spoke in Mandarin. 'It is well known that all toys slump, and slumping and wisdom never go together. Either you slump, or you are wise — you can't have both. That's why there is no point in asking toys about wisdom, and where it comes from, and all those things. We owls know this.'

With that, Ted returned home to the toys in the other corner of the bedroom. He worried all the way about what Han Owl had said. If he was to be comfortable, he needed to slump. Yet if he was wise he shouldn't slump, because if he did, everybody would think he had no wisdom. Could it be possible to be comfortable and wise as well?

Back in his corner, the toys greeted him as if he had returned from a long, heroic journey, and he told them all that had happened with the owls.

When he had completely finished, all the toys settled down again as if nothing had happened. From then on, though, they noticed that Ted was not slumping as much as before, and he appeared to be further lost in thought than ever.

It even seemed to some that he had decided to arrange himself in such a way that he might be expected to answer questions, give advice and sometimes make judgements.